Siberian Tigers

by Grace Hansen

Abdo Kids Jumbo is an Imprint of Abdo Kids
abdopublishing.com

abdopublishing.com

Published by Abdo Kids, a division of ABDO, P.O. Box 398166, Minneapolis, Minnesota 55439.
Copyright © 2019 by Abdo Consulting Group, Inc. International copyrights reserved in all countries.
No part of this book may be reproduced in any form without written permission from the publisher.
Abdo Kids Jumbo™ is a trademark and logo of Abdo Kids.

052018
092018

 THIS BOOK CONTAINS RECYCLED MATERIALS

Photo Credits: iStock, Minden Pictures, Shutterstock

Production Contributors: Teddy Borth, Jennie Forsberg, Grace Hansen

Design Contributors: Dorothy Toth, Laura Mitchell

Library of Congress Control Number: 2017960568
Publisher's Cataloging-in-Publication Data

Names: Hansen, Grace, author.
Title: Siberian tigers / by Grace Hansen.
Description: Minneapolis, Minnesota : Abdo Kids, 2019. | Series: Super species |
    Includes glossary, index and online resources (page 24).
Identifiers: ISBN 9781532108266 (lib.bdg.) | ISBN 9781532109249 (ebook) |
    ISBN 9781532109737 (Read-to-me ebook)
Subjects: LCSH: Siberian tiger--Juvenile literature. | Body size--Juvenile literature. |
    Animals--Size--Juvenile literature. | Animal behavior--Juvenile literature.
Classification: DDC 599.756--dc23

Table of Contents

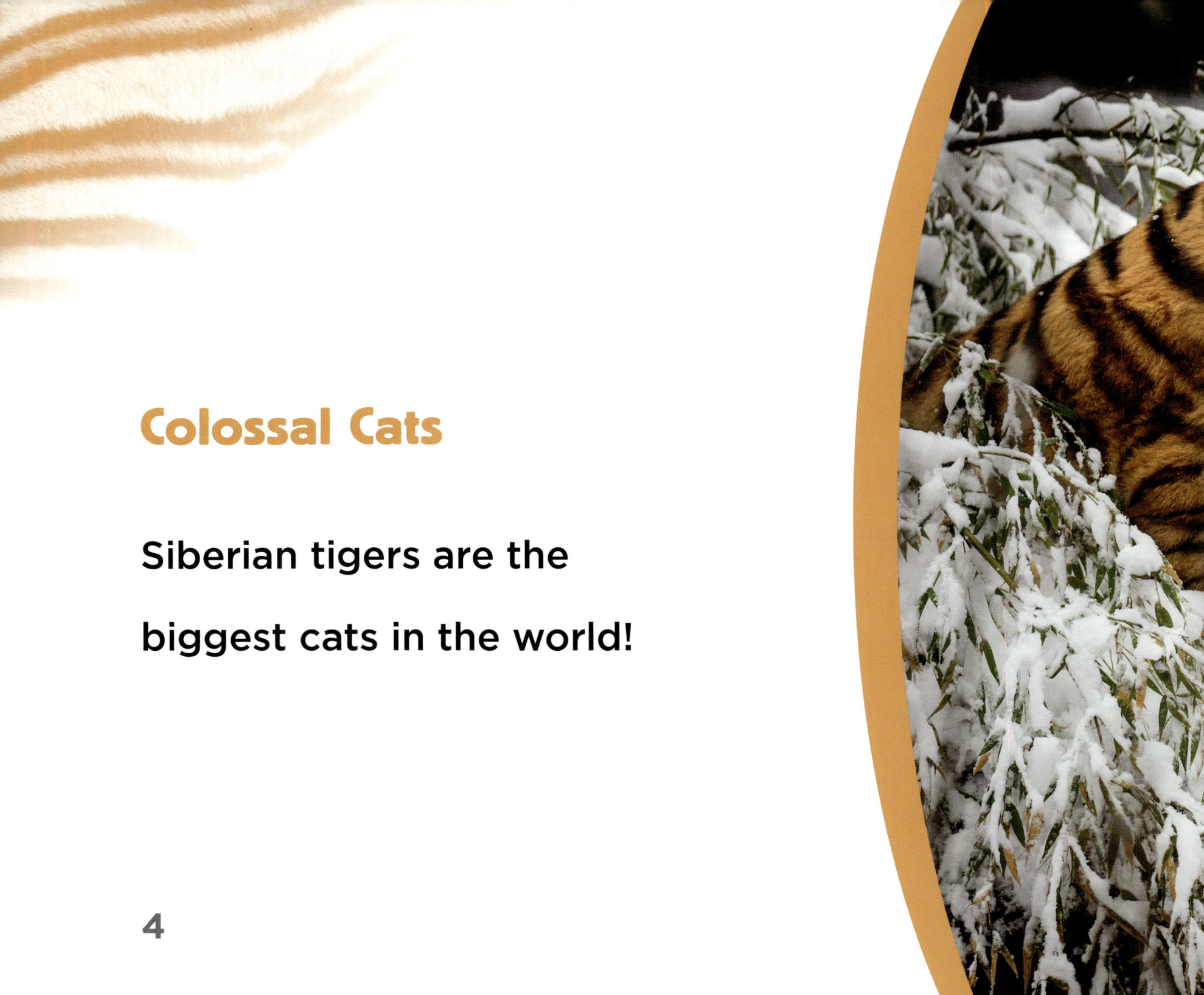

Colossal Cats

Siberian tigers are the biggest cats in the world!

4

They mainly live in forests

in parts of Russia.

Male Siberian tigers are

much larger than females.

Males can grow up to 12 feet (3.7 m) long. That is the same length as two male lions!

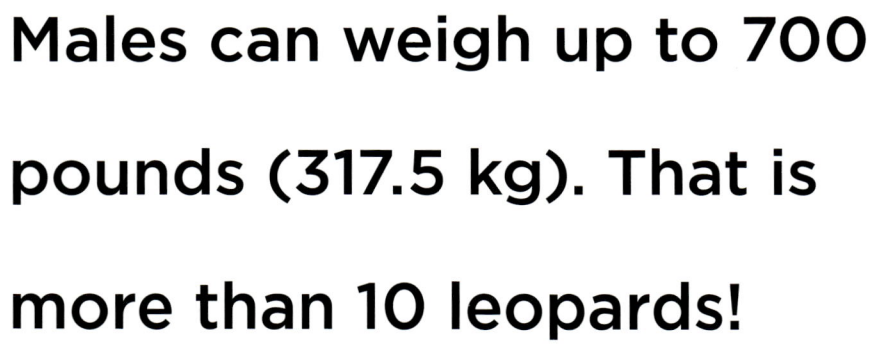

Males can weigh up to 700 pounds (317.5 kg). That is more than 10 leopards!

Siberian tiger

leopards

13

Siberian tigers are covered in thick, warm **fur**. It can grow more than 4 inches (10.2 cm) long!

Hunting

Hungry Siberian tigers hunt at night. They can eat up to 60 pounds (27.2 kg) in one night!

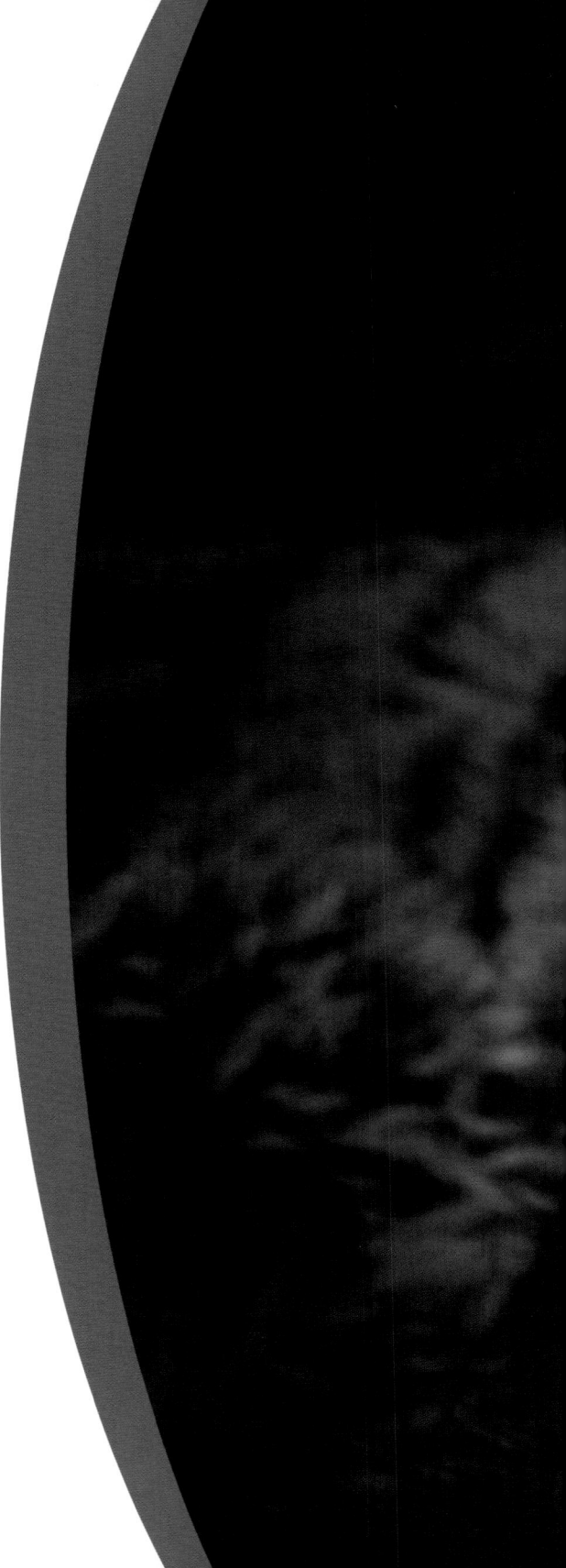

Siberian Cubs

Female Siberian tigers have 2 to 6 **cubs**. They give birth once every two years.

Siberian tiger cubs weigh

about 3.5 pounds (1.6 kg)

at birth. But they grow fast!

They can help their mothers

hunt at around 18 months old.

More Facts

- A Siberian tiger's tail can grow up to 3 feet (91.4 cm) long!

- Siberian tigers are on average becoming smaller. This is because they have less space and food.

- A Siberian tiger that was raised in **captivity** grew to be 1,025 pounds (464.9 kg)!

Glossary

captivity – the situation in which an animal is kept somewhere and is cared for by humans.

cub – a baby tiger.

fur – the soft, thick hair that covers the bodies of certain animals.

Index

Abdo Kids
ONLINE
FREE! ONLINE MULTIMEDIA RESOURCES

Visit **abdokids.com** and use this code to access crafts, games, videos, and more!

Abdo Kids Code:
SSK8266